AF434892

Love

A Collection of Prose and Poetry

by

Puja Mohan

The journey of finding true love begins with first loving oneself unconditionally.

for you

Love Notes

Close to my Heart

I have scars
that you cannot see.
They tell a tale
of how strong
I have been.

I have loved
and I have lost.

I have scars.

I wear them
here
close to my heart.

Heart

Stay
you say.
Leave
says my heart.

Stay
you say.
Forget
says my heart.

Stay
you say.

Nothing says my heart.

Fooled

I am not fooled
by what I see in the mirror.
The scars
the lines
they remind me of my past.

I am not fooled
by what I see in the mirror.

What makes you think
I will be fooled
by your
love yous.

Saving

You need me to save you
from yourself.
He said.
Contempt laced every word.

Saving.
No
I don't need a man to save me.
Least of all from myself.

I don't need you to save me.
I need to save myself

above all from your love.

Piece by piece

This was inevitable.
I sit here gathering my stuff
piece by piece I pack my love.

We've been together a long time now.
Years have come and years have gone.

They say love is enough
but not for us.

The fissures in our heart
grew wider each day.

Until all the love
seeped away.

Before we lose
the respect we have.

I sit here gathering my stuff
piece by piece I pack my love.

You were never mine

I wish to be a magician
then I would bring you back.

I wish to be a temptress
then I would keep you forever.

You were never mine to begin with.
You are not mine in the end.

Scars

I've been in love
a few times now.

I wore my heart
on my sleeves.

And now
I wear its scar.

For love 

I was naïve.

Hours you spent
making me feel
I am not enough
I mistook it
for love.

I look away

No
I don't love you.
I look away
worried you'll catch the lie.

What I should have said
that day was
Yes
I love you.

Instead
I spent a lifetime
pretending
I didn't.

He said

You are not enough
he said.

You are not pretty enough.
You are not wealthy enough.
You are not intelligent enough.
You are not worthy enough.
You are not enough
he said.

It took him awhile
to recognize me.
Years had gone by.

It's you
he said.
His eyes betrayed his stoic face.
You've done well for yourself
he said.
A compliment laced with regret.

Thank you
I said.
I was strong enough.

To You

I am sorry
to have not loved you.
I am sorry
to have allowed the abuse.
I am sorry
to have watched you wilt way.

To you
I am sorry
my beautiful self.

The healing
can now begin.

I changed

Every time I fell in love
I changed.
To be what you wanted.
To show you I was worthy

of your love.

I have risen in love.
I changed.
To be what I always was.
To show I was worthy

of my love.

Once again

I catch myself smiling a lot.
I see myself more clearly in the mirror.
I've been humming that song
for a week now.
And still I can go on.
I am kinder to myself
than I have been in years.
I see more lines around my lips.

Once again
I am in love
with myself.

My heart

What is it
my heart?

Just a moment
when the hurt you gave
does not ache.

What is it
my heart?

Just a moment
when the joy you gave
does not ache.

I will find

You have broken my heart
one too many times.
But you cannot break my spirit.

It'll take a while.
My strength will come back.
I will love again.

And this time
I will find.

A funny way

Love
has a funny way
of finding you.

You can close your heart.
But it finds a way
through those very cracks
that have made you fear
love.

In Love

Someday
when you least expect.

Quietly it will reach for you
when you least suspect.

And you'll find yourself
in love.

Hush...

You cannot love without fear.
It whispers a million doubts.

Hush...
There is nothing worth having
without a little risk.

Hush...
I'll be fine even with a broken heart.

Hush...
I'll find love even when it's dark.

Hush...
I'll find love even with a broken heart.

Love is a process

Love
Is a process
Not the final destination

It is exciting in the beginning
Rewarding towards the end
But messy in the middle

And that is its true test.

Gone Awhile

I don't love you
Any less
But you've been gone
Awhile

Finally I see the light
At the end of this tunnel
The ache you left
behind

A new life
Ready to happen
To me
I don't love you
Any less
But you've been gone
Awhile.

He said

My heart is cold
The frost will not melt

Take your love
It needs warmth to blossom

Love needs nothing
It holds all the warmth it needs
wrapped neatly inside
He said

My heart is no more cold
The frost has melted away

Love is what I needed

I am glad
He said.

You came along

I have always been fearless
Never afraid to love
And then you came along
And wiped away my pretenses
And now I know
I have always been fearful
Never really loved
And then
You came along.

Old Love

I gave up on love
Long ago
It was not meant for me

Or I was not meant for it
I will never know

Then you walked into my life
And there was an old familiarity
In our new love

I was made of love
You came and showed me how.

Rest of our lives

There I saw
What I had never seen in any lover of
mine

In his eyes
Was not love
But
Respect

We had the rest of our lives
To fall
In love.

Broken Promise

I will never love again
I promise you this

Our parting words
Feel heavy today

I had caged the beast
who longed to be freed
I will never love again
I promised you this

A marriage was there
But my love
Was with you

I never knew
My heart could love another
For unconditional was his

The beast is out
I am sorry for the
Broken promise.

Into my life

You walked into my life
Not when I wanted you
But when I needed you.

Today

I wish to go back in time
And save me a whole lot of heartaches
But that will alter
The unconditional love
I feel for him today.

In that moment

When did I know
I was in love
You ask

It's when
I let go
But
You held on

I knew
In that moment
I'll forever
Love this man.

Also available by Puja Mohan

Fiction

Perfect Imperfections

Meant to be

Nonfiction

I am a Goal Digger
(Book 1 in Goal Digger Series)

Goals, From Start to Success
(Book 2 in Goal Digger Series)

My 90-Day Plan
(Book 3 in Goal Digger Series)

About the Author

Puja grew up in Bokaro before going to a boarding school in Panchgani at the age of twelve where she developed her love for books and even dabbled a little in writing short stories.

As a graduate with a dual degree in Management (Marketing Communications & Human Resource), she jump-started her career in project control & finance and has almost seven years of experience working for a multinational corporation. She now lives in California with her husband and her son and is currently dedicating her time to her writing and her family. When she is not writing, you can find her reading or explore the city.

Read more about her at www.pujamohan.com
Or follow her on Instagram – Puja.Mohan
Twitter – MohanPuja
Facebook – Puja Mohan

www.ingramcontent.com/pod-product-compliance
Lightning Source LLC
Chambersburg PA
CBHW021401160726

47994CB00007B/3045